Dedications

For my son Luca, forever a light in my life.
I look forward to teaching you how to ride a bicycle
so we can enjoy rides together. – Maria

For my Dad, former British professional cyclist
Bob Chadwick, who always has exciting bicycle race
tales to retell. – Zoe

Published in Australia 2022
by Bonny Books
ABN 34 130 323 793
www.mariamonte.com

Copyright © 2022 Maria Monte
Cover and illustrations by Zoe Saunders

A Cataloging-in-Publication entry for this book is
available from the National Library of Australia.

ISBN: 978-0-9875130-6-9 (Paperback)
ISBN: 978-0-9875130-7-6 (Hardcover)

Ellery's Magic Bicycle

Story by Maria Monte   Illustrations by Zoe Saunders

One day, Ellery found an old purple bicycle.

Suddenly, it sprung up and—**thwack!**—shook off the mud, dints, and rust.

The bicycle circled Ellery who spun around, chasing it with excitement and wonder.

"Come with me?" Ellery asked, hopefully.

The bicycle sped to her side,
and they went home together.

"Teach me?" Ellery asked the next day.

The bicycle helped her along. Ellery frowned as she tried to balance. The bicycle's bell brought her smile back by sounding like an old bullfrog
–ruhdoop!

"Play with me!" Ellery laughed.

They spent many afternoons together
by the pond.

Ellery made daisy chains and mud pies
while singing rhymes.

When Ellery grew too big for the bicycle, it wiggled and—thwump!—grew bigger.

As Ellery kept growing, so did the bicycle.

A boy named Charlie and his family moved in next door.

Ellery ran to say hello, but he did not want to make friends.

"Protect me!" cried Ellery as Charlie threw pebbles.

Ellery's bicycle stood between them, the stones clink, clink, clinking against its frame.

Ellery bandaged her bicycle's dints.

The next day, Ellery threw mud pies at Charlie for hurting her bicycle.

When he ran away, she felt sorry and decided to make it right.

"Help me," pleaded Ellery.

So, the bicycle let Charlie have a ride.

From then on, all three were best friends.

Years later, Charlie's family moved away. The night before leaving, Charlie crept to the bike shed. There, he tied a basket to the bicycle as a surprise for Ellery.

Pink and yellow flowers sprouted right before his eyes! Charlie gave the bicycle a thumbs-up, and it replied with a proud hop.

"Hold me," sobbed Ellery the next day,
heartbroken that Charlie was gone.

Ellery clung to her bicycle, her tears tap, tap,
tapping against its frame. It softened against
Ellery's face and felt like a pillow.

Ellery became a daredevil teenager.

"Fly with me!" she squealed.

They ploughed through hedges, dashed through ditches, and soared off ramps.

As years passed, Ellery only had time for quick rides at sunrise.

"Let's exercise," she would mutter.

Finally, Ellery stopped asking anything
of the bicycle.

Tiny spiders surfed their stringy webs on the bicycle's spokes.

One morning, the bicycle saw Ellery and Charlie with their baby. They were singing the same rhymes Ellery had sung to the bicycle long ago.

Whirr, the bicycle's wheels spun cheerfully now that its friends were together again.

The baby grew into a bright girl. The bicycle
wanted to join her. It rang its bell,
but no one listened.

The bicycle gave up and fell asleep.

Charlie brought home a new bicycle.

One spring, Ellery and Charlie cleared out the shed, getting ready for their junk to be collected.

They were all together again, but the bicycle stayed silent.

Ellery stared at the bicycle for the longest time.
Then the rubbish van arrived.

The bicycle shivered and made a final plea
with a faint ting-a-ling.

Smiling, Ellery whispered, "Stay with me."

About Maria

Maria Monte writes sweet, heart-warming, and fun stories that inspire a love of learning and teach children great values, such as kindness and love. Maria lives with her young son in Melbourne, Australia. She is an experienced communications specialist with an honours degree in English literature.

You can connect with Maria via her website, www.mariamonte.com.

About Zoe

Zoe Saunders lives in Cheshire, UK, with her son, daughter and husband. She has always had a love of artistry, and likes to sketch, paint and create sweet characters in her whimsical style. She is particularly fascinated by animals, both real and magical, and adores painting natural scenery and foliage. Zoe creates her artwork using either traditional pen and watercolor, or digitally with her iPad Pro.

You can connect with Zoe via her website, www.whimsicolourart.com.

CPSIA information can be obtained
at www.ICGtesting.com
Printed in the USA
BVHW021004140622
639652BV00020B/164